LOST!

LOST!

PATTI TRIMBLE

ILLUSTRATED BY DANIEL MORETON

Green Light Readers
Harcourt, Inc.

Orlando   Austin   New York   San Diego   Toronto   London

"I'm lost," said Gil the ant.

"Where am I?
It's so wet in here."

"I will walk up," said Gil.

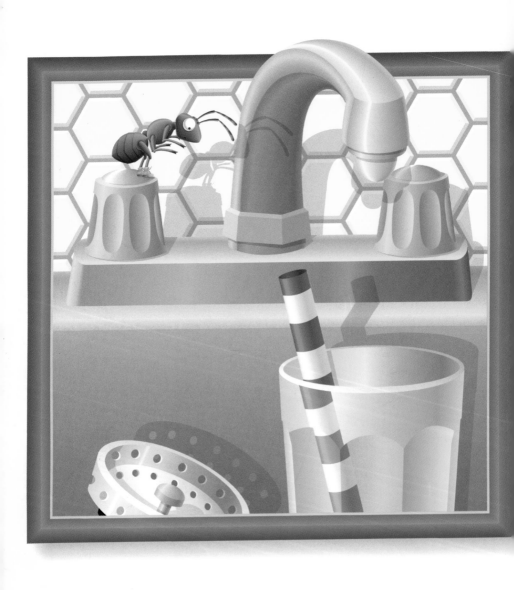

"Now I see.
I was in a sink!"

"What is this?" said Gil.
"It's a big two."

"Oh, it's a clock!"

"Now all I see is pink!" Gil said.
"I will walk on and on."

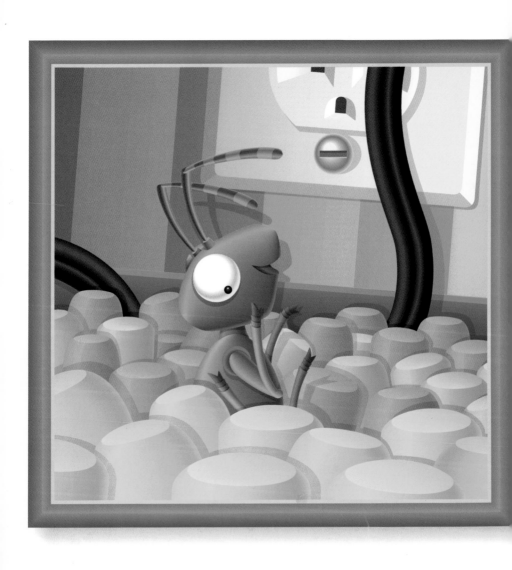

"Oh, it's a pink mat!"

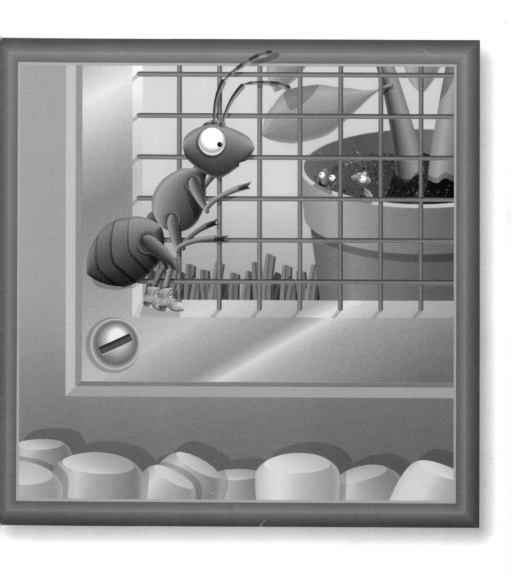

"Help!" called Gil, the lost ant.

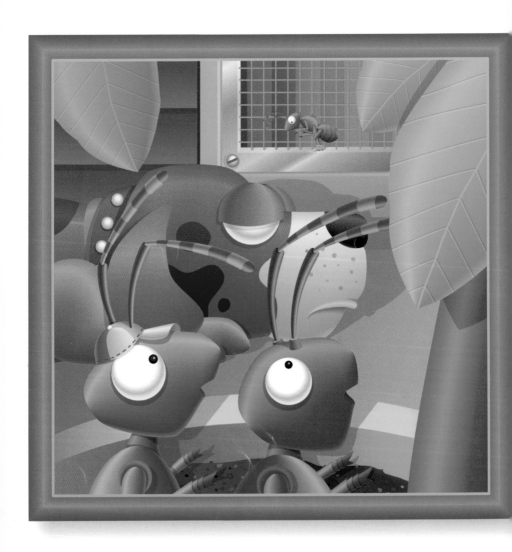

"Sneak past that dog," called his two friends.

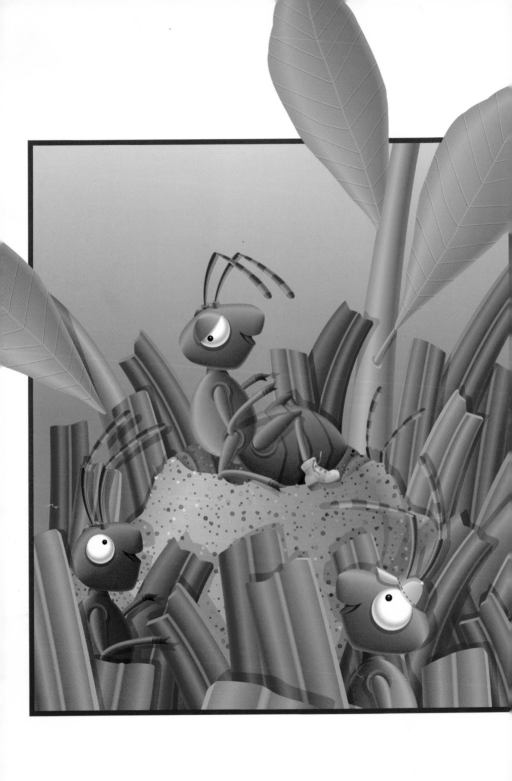

"Whew!" said Gil.
"I'm glad to be home!"

ANT
BOOKMARK

Gil was lost.

Make a bookmark so
you are never lost
when you are
reading a book.

paper

crayons or markers

scissors

glue

1. Draw an ant at the top of your bookmark.

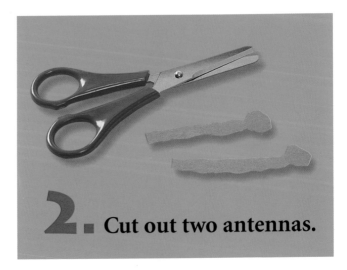

2. Cut out two antennas.

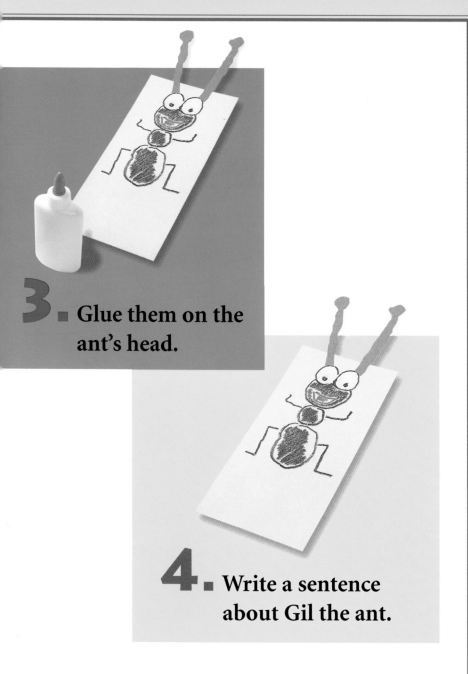

3. Glue them on the ant's head.

4. Write a sentence about Gil the ant.

Share your bookmark with a friend!

Meet the Illustrator

Daniel Moreton loved listening to his
grandmother's stories when he was a child.
They made him want to write stories and
books of his own. He also creates pictures
for his books. He uses a computer to draw
them, just as he did for this story about
Gil the ant. He hopes his stories inspire
you to write stories, too!

www.HarcourtBooks.com

First Green Light Readers edition 2000
Green Light Readers is a trademark of Harcourt, Inc., registered in the
United States of America and/or other jurisdictions.

The Library of Congress has cataloged an earlier edition as follows:
Trimble, Patti.
Lost!/Patti Trimble; illustrated by Daniel Moreton.
p. cm.
"Green Light Readers."
Summary: After having been lost in a sink and among unfamiliar objects, Gil the
ant sneaks past a dog and finally finds his way home.
[1. Ants—Fiction.] I. Moreton, Daniel, ill. II. Title.
PZ7.T73525Lo 2000
[E]—dc21   99-50809
ISBN 0-15-204824-3
ISBN 0-15-204864-2 (pb)

A C E G H F D B
A C E G H F D B (pb)

Ages 4-6
Grades: K-1
Guided Reading Level: C-D
Reading Recovery Level: 6-7

Green Light Readers
For the reader who's ready to GO!

"A must-have for any family with a beginning reader."—*Boston Sunday Herald*

"You can't go wrong with adding several copies of these terrific books to your beginning-to-read collection."—*School Library Journal*

"A winner for the beginner."—*Booklist*

Five Tips to Help Your Child Become a Great Reader

1. Get involved. Reading aloud to and with your child is just as important as encouraging your child to read independently.

2. Be curious. Ask questions about what your child is reading.

3. Make reading fun. Allow your child to pick books on subjects that interest her or him.

4. Words are everywhere—not just in books. Practice reading signs, packages, and cereal boxes with your child.

5. Set a good example. Make sure your child sees YOU reading.

Why Green Light Readers Is the Best Series for Your New Reader

• Created exclusively for beginning readers by some of the biggest and brightest names in children's books

• Reinforces the reading skills your child is learning in school

• Encourages children to read—and finish—books by themselves

• Offers extra enrichment through fun, age-appropriate activities unique to each story

• Incorporates characteristics of the Reading Recovery program used by educators

• Developed with Harcourt School Publishers and credentialed educational consultants

DATE DUE

MAR 23			
APR 28			
JAN 25			
FEB 08			
FEB 14			
FEB 01			
MAR 14			
DEC 18			